D0933582

HALF SPENT
Was the
NIGHT

AMI
MᶜKAY

HALF SPENT
~ Was the ~
NIGHT

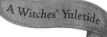

A Witches' Yuletide

ALFRED A. KNOPF CANADA

PUBLISHED BY ALFRED A. KNOPF CANADA

Copyright © 2018 Ami McKay

www.penguinrandomhouse.ca

Knopf Canada and colophon are registered trademarks.

Library and Archives Canada Cataloguing in Publication

McKay, Ami, 1968–, author
     Half spent was the night : a witches' yuletide / Ami McKay.

Issued in print and electronic formats.
ISBN 978-0-7352-7566-9
eBook ISBN 978-0-7352-7567-6

     I. Title.

PS8625.K387H35 2018   C813'.6   C2018-901806-2
                                                C2018-901807-0

Book design by Kelly Hill

Cover images: (paper background) © MagicDogWorkshop, (flourishes) © Vasya Kobelev, both Shutterstock.com; (holly) © CSA Images/ B&W Icon Collection, (crow) © Andrew_Howe, (mask) © cienpies, (scrolls) © Yayasya, all Getty Images; (moon) "Partial eclipse of the moon. Observed October 24, 1874." from The Trouvelot astronomical drawings by E. L. Trouvelot. From the New York Public Library.

Endpaper image © Elena Paletskaya / Shutterstock.com

Interior images: (bread) © Sketch Master, (card) © Picsfive, (elderberry) © cuttlefish84, (owl) © Bodor Tivadar, (paper) © Tomas Jasinskis, (flowers) © Eisfrei, all Shutterstock.com; (chestnut, moth, teapot, teacup) from 3,800 Early Advertising Cuts © Dover Publications, Inc.; (fox) from Scan This Book © John Mendenhall.

Printed and bound in the United States of America

10 9 8 7 6 5 4 3 2 1

For the Grandmothers,
who carried winter's
magic in their hearts.

HALF

SPENT

WAS

THE

NIGHT

DECEMBER 29, 1881

Christmas Day has come and gone, the New Year lies ahead. Strange things happen Between the Years, in the days outside of time. Minutes go wild, hours vanish. Idleness becomes a clever thief, stealing the names of the days of the week, muting the steady tick of watches and clocks. These are the hours when angels, ghosts, demons and meddlers ride howling wind and flickering candlelight, keen to stir unguarded hearts and restless minds.

Tonight, the three Witches of New York, swathed in dressing gowns of velvet and silk, are seated on tasseled pillows before a crackling fire.

They've set the business of potions, spells and con-
sultations aside, in favour of quiet contemplation.
The youngest, Beatrice, touchstone of spirits, is
curious and bright-eyed. The eldest, Eleanor,
keeper of spells, is watchful, regal and wise.
Adelaide, seer of fate, sits between them, ever
ready to speak her mind. Bellies full of honey
cake and hot cider, they seek comfort, warmth,
companionship and glimpses of the future.

Beatrice scores a chestnut with a small knife
to prepare it for roasting. "My aunt Lydia always
said a cracked nut means 'yes,' and one that burns
without cracking means 'no.'" The fire hisses and
pops. A spark flies into the air and lands on the
hearth where it pulses, then dies. After placing
her chestnut in a shallow pan, she sets the pan on
the fire and waits for an answer.

Eleanor watches with anticipation. So does
Perdu, her raven familiar.

The bird is keen for the sweet roasted meat of
the nut. Eleanor, for a morsel of truth. She knows
Beatrice is keeping a secret.

A faint *yessss* sounds before the chestnut

squeals and its shell blossoms in an attempt to turn itself inside out.

Eleanor stares at her young apprentice. *Is she happy, sad or indifferent at these portents?*

Tugging at her braid, Beatrice bites her lip, then smiles when she realizes how closely she's being watched.

"Pleased?" Adelaide asks, fishing for the truth she knows Eleanor wants to uncover.

Beatrice doesn't answer. Nor does she meet the eyes of her companions.

Distracted or determined, Eleanor wonders. *Which is it?*

Neither. The girl is mulling over the answer she's received. *Yes,* she thinks, *but when?* For weeks she's been ravenous with longing for a stranger she's only seen in her dreams. It isn't love, exactly. How could it be? It's more a relentless curiosity. She would follow the Stranger anywhere. And she has, on many nights, chasing his dark figure through dimly lit corridors and graveyards bathed in moonlight. In the morning she wakes exhausted, wishing she could go back to sleep, desperate to return to the last place she saw him. Even if she could explain her state to her friends, she wouldn't. She's afraid that once she gives voice to her vision, the Stranger will disappear from her mind forever. Whenever she attempts to write an account of her dreams, his voice sounds in her head: *Don't break the spell*. It leaves her puzzled, intrigued. Are the fay-folk Eleanor so often speaks of the source of these visions? Or do they come from someplace else? The girl has plied herself with many cups of dream tea, offered countless trinkets made of mother-of-pearl and coloured glass in order to persuade the fickle creatures to bring her answers, all to no avail. *How long must I continue the chase?* At least now (if the humble chestnut is to be believed), she knows she's destined to meet the Stranger in the flesh. *Even if I don't know the how or why of it.*

Picking the chestnut from the pan, she deftly peels the shell from the meat. It's piping hot but she's not concerned with getting burned. She's thinking instead of the Stranger, of how soon she can go to sleep and find him in her dreams.

Holding the fleshy heart of the nut in the palm of her hand until it cools, she offers it to Perdu.

"Who's a good bird?" the raven coos before snatching the treat in his beak.

"What if yes or no isn't enough?" Eleanor asks. She wants Beatrice to perform another divination. Maybe then she'll be able to figure out what's on the girl's mind.

"If you need to choose between different situations," Beatrice replies, "you must name each chestnut according to your choices, then kiss them for luck before putting them into the fire. The order in which they burst is either the order in which you must address the issues or the way in which things will ultimately come to pass."

"Situations, or *suitors*?" Adelaide teases. She's noticed Beatrice growing more preoccupied by the day—moving about like a sleepwalker, twirling her hair with absent-minded vigour. She's convinced the girl is having a secret affair. She knows the blush of lust when she sees it. *Good for her,* she thinks. *If only Eleanor would stop worrying and leave Beatrice to it.*

Attempting to save the girl from further scrutiny, Adelaide takes three chestnuts from the bowl and deftly cuts an X into each one. Then touching the knife to them one by one, she proclaims, "I dub thee Rum, Brandy and Schnapps." Her own beloved, Dr. Brody, is away until the New Year, leading a delegation from the Unknown Philosophers' Society at a conference on psychical research. When he comes home, he'll be expecting her answer to the weighty question he'd asked before he left. *Will you marry me?* Puckering her lips, Adelaide delivers a kiss to each nut before placing them in the pan. She'd much rather play with what she should drink tonight than think on *yes*, *no* or *maybe*.

Beatrice offers the bowl of fresh chestnuts to Eleanor. "Would you like to give it a try? It's a silly old tradition, but it's fun." She doesn't expect the wise hedge witch to take her aunt's lowly form of divination seriously, especially not when Eleanor comes from such a storied lineage of natural magic, and she herself, from none. Roasting chestnuts is certainly no match for Eleanor's tea-leaf readings or Adelaide's tarot cards, but the three women have made a pact to take a break from their duties and their clients during the holidays, even putting a sign in the window of their tea-shop, the Hermitage, that reads: CLOSED UNTIL THE NEW YEAR.

Eleanor, as usual, is having difficulty finding her way to lightheartedness. "Every superstition contains truth," she responds. "The trick is in finding it."

Setting the bowl on the table, Beatrice leaves the choice to her mentor. She knows better than to cajole her.

A derisive scoffing noise from behind them startles the women. None of the witches had seen Dr. Brody's housekeeper, Mrs. Stutt, settle in a nearby chair with her knitting.

"Gesundheit, Mrs. Stutt," Adelaide says. Then adds, sharply, "Don't you ever take a night off?"

Stowing her knitting in a basket, the elderly woman gets up out of her chair and glares at Adelaide as she leaves the room.

8   AMI MCKAY

"Why must you be so rude to her?" Eleanor whispers to Adelaide. The eldest witch was far more inclined to be sympathetic toward Mrs. Stutt than her sword-tongued friend.

The housekeeper had experienced quite a shock when her long-time employer, Dr. Brody, had welcomed the three witches into his home the previous year. Mrs. Stutt had tended to every scrape, bruise and nightmare he'd had as a boy and her instinct to protect him has never waned. In the past few months, she's come to trust Eleanor and Beatrice, but warming up to Adelaide has proved more difficult, largely because the beautiful if scarred one-eyed witch has so clearly won the doctor's heart.

"It's not as if she's ever been very welcoming to me," Adelaide complains.

Eleanor shakes her head. "I wouldn't say that. She tolerates you as well as the rest of us do."

"Tolerates," Adelaide says with a smirk. "I really must work harder to earn her loathing."

Beatrice feigns a yawn, angling to excuse herself so she can go to bed and dream.

As the intoxicating scent of roasting chest-nuts rises from the pan, the middle nut in the trio that represents Adelaide's dilemma begins to hiss. Letting go a sharp squeak, it cracks and pops.

"Hello, Brandy!" Adelaide says as she rises from the floor and heads to the liquor cabinet. Taking bottle and snifter in hand, she prepares to pour. Then she pauses and asks, "Anyone care to join me?"

"Sure," Eleanor replies. "But just a finger."

"None for me," Beatrice says, getting up. "I'm turning in for the night."

Before the young witch can make her escape, Mrs. Stutt returns with an odd assortment of kitchen wares—a copper saucepan half full of water, a long-handled ladle, and a glass jar filled with lead buttons, tokens, fishing weights and buckshot. "I am to show you *Bleigiessen*," she says, placing each item on the table.

"Blei-gies-sen," Beatrice says, trying to make sense of the word.

"Does it come with sauerkraut?" Adelaide teases.

"Hush," Eleanor scolds.

Mrs. Stutt frowns. "It is the proper way to see your fate."

Plucking a sprig of holly from a garland draped over the mantle, she feeds it to the fire then reaches for the bellows. Elbows pumping, she brings the flames to renewed vigour. The light of the fire dances on her face, casting an eerie red glow over her hair and wrinkled cheeks. She calls to the sparks as she works, whispering to them in an ancient form of her native tongue. "*Ben zi bena, bluot si bluoda . . .*" She alone knows the meaning of her words: *bone to bone, blood to blood.*

Adelaide stalks toward Mrs. Stutt, clearly ready to chase her away.

Eleanor stops her with a look.

Setting the bellows aside, Mrs. Stutt turns to the witches. "It is a grave mistake to tell a god how to make up her mind. She will speak to you in the dead days before the New Year, but only through fire and shadow. Not like an organ-grinder's monkey pointing to whichever shell hides the pea."

Adelaide says, "Aren't you full of surprises."

"Youngest first," the housekeeper says, and hands the ladle to Beatrice. Then she directs the girl to place several bits of lead into its bowl and hold the ladle over the hottest part of the fire. "Once the metal has changed to liquid, you pour it into the pot of water."

Eleanor is enthralled; this form of divination is completely new to her.

Beatrice watches with wonder as the bits of metal dissolve into each other to form a shimmering pool of molten lead.

Placing the copper pot on the hearth, Mrs. Stutt says, "Now give it to the water without any hesitation in your heart."

Beatrice holds her breath as she pours the lead into the pot. In an instant, the glistening liquid has frozen solid, as if seized by an invisible force. "Oh!' she exclaims, eyes wide, afraid to touch the shiny, newborn object.

Mrs. Stutt fishes out the lump. "Here," she says, placing it on the table for all to see.

Beatrice squints at it. "What am I supposed to do with it?"

"We give it to the shadows," Mrs. Stutt says.

With that, a knock sounds at door.

Beatrice says, "You all stay put. I'll answer."

Perdu hops to the floor to escort her.

Beatrice opens the door to find a messenger dressed in livery from another time—powdered wig, tricorn hat, black velvet knickers, damask vest, and a long wool coat of brilliant blue trimmed with lush embroidery. "Delivery for Miss Beatrice Dunn," he announces, as he pulls an envelope from his coat pocket.

"I'm she," Beatrice, says. "I mean, Miss Dunn is me."

Hard snow slants at the young man's back as his breath clouds in the frigid air. His cheeks are ruddy with cold, his nose dripping. Perdu watches him with a curious stare.

Adelaide joins Beatrice at the door and takes pity on the messenger. "Would you like to come inside for a moment and warm yourself by the fire?" Swirling her drink in the bowl of her snifter, she adds, "Perhaps you'd like some brandy?"

"No thank you, ma'am," he replies with a slight bow.

Fishing a coin from her pocket, Beatrice hands it to the messenger. "Goodnight," she says, clutching the envelope as she closes the door.

Just as she is about to break the wax seal on her missive, all the lights in the house flicker, and a second knock sounds.

"Perhaps he's changed his mind," Adelaide says, opening the door.

"Perhaps he wants a bigger tip," Eleanor mutters, joining her sister witches in the foyer.

The second messenger is dressed in the same antiquated manner as the first, except his coat is yellow. "Delivery for Miss Adelaide Thom," he announces, presenting a second envelope.

"You really should confer with your compatriot," Adelaide says as she plucks the envelope from his hand.

Perdu tugs at Eleanor's skirts as she steps up to hand the second messenger his tip.

"Thank you, ma'am," he says, and disappears into the blustery night.

As she closes the door behind him, Adelaide says to Beatrice, "Don't open yours just yet." And with that, a third knock sounds. Turning to Eleanor she says, "I believe this one will be for you."

The third messenger is dressed in deep scarlet. "Delivery for Miss Eleanor St. Clair."

"Of course."

Perdu chortles and flaps about as his mistress accepts the note.

When they are sure the third messenger has gone, the three witches poke their heads outside the door and peer into the night. Snow falls heavy and fast, every house, carriage and street lamp disappearing in the churning blizzard. All they can hear is the faint sound of dogs barking against the howling wind.

YOU ARE CORDIALLY INVITED TO

A RAUHNÄCHT MASQUERADE

to mark the revels of Yuletide.

DECEMBER 31, 1881

8 O'CLOCK *to* NEW YEAR'S DAY

in the GRAND BALLROOM

of the

FIFTH AVENUE HOTEL

RSVP BY NOON, DECEMBER 31ST,

at the FIFTH AVENUE HOTEL.

IN PERSON ONLY. NO EXCEPTIONS.

DONATIONS WILL BE SOLICITED ON BEHALF

of the FOUNDATION FOR LOST CHILDREN.

BARONESS BERTA WEISSHIRSCH, HEAD TRUSTEE.

Out with the old. In with the new.

Beatrice smooths her invitation between her fingers, then holds it to her nose. It smells like cinnamon, ginger and clove. The other two witches' invitations are the same.

"It's awfully short notice, isn't it?" Eleanor asks. "As far as these things go."

Adelaide considers the fine quality of the paper, the skill of the calligrapher's hand. "Whoever this Baroness is, she spares no expense. My guess is that she can do what she likes because she's used to people doing whatever she asks of them."

"Does that mean you're going?" Beatrice asks.

"What else have I got to do?" Adelaide replies. "Besides, I'm always keen to meet a woman like that."

Beatrice looks at Eleanor. "And you?"

"I don't know. Probably not."

"Well I'm going," Beatrice says, flushed with excitement. She believes the invitation not only confirms the response she got from the chestnut, but that it will lead her to the *where* and *when* of it. "I wouldn't miss it for the world."

While the witches talk of balls and baronesses, Mrs. Stutt sits forgotten in the parlour, regarding the homely lump of lead. With a candle in her other hand, she holds Beatrice's *Bleigiessen* near the wall and coaxes the girl's fate from the shadows the object casts.

What she sees frightens her beyond measure. No matter which way she turns the lump a dark figure appears before her—a demon's face with gaping mouth and flashing eyes.

Heart racing, she pockets the lump, gathers the tools of her craft and scurries back to the kitchen. If they forgot her in the parlour, perhaps they'll forget her misguided attempt at witchery as well. *Maybe it's a mistake*, she thinks. *A symptom of my age.*

Her heart knows better. The girl is in danger.

DECEMBER 30

The storm subsides. The day begins. For a brief while in the early morning, the city is a perfect winter scene—church steeples and storefronts flocked and frosted, sidewalks and streets made clean and new—a snow globe at rest in Nature's hands.

Beatrice and Adelaide make their way to the Fifth Avenue Hotel just after breakfast, cutting through Madison Square Park as they go to deliver their replies. Every shrub, tree and lamp post shines in the dazzling sunlight. Children break free from their mothers' hands to whirl around them, kicking up the snow. Each impish bundle of wool and laughter fills the witches' hearts with longing. Beatrice, for a childhood barely passed. Adelaide, for the one she never had.

Someone watches as they stroll by, along with all the other unnoticed creatures that inhabit the place. Bird, squirrel, fox, hare, spirits without home or flesh.

Look,

　　Listen,

　　　　See.

Hear.

　　　　Behold,

　　　　Beware…

Witches!

When they arrive at the hotel, they're greeted by every doorman, bellhop and maid they pass. Adelaide, by the present staff, who know her well as hotel owner Marietta Stevens' favourite fortune teller. Beatrice, by the dearly departed, who know it is the girl's particular gift to see the dead.

"Good morning, Miss Thom."

"Good day, Miss Dunn."

"Good to see you, Miss Thom."

"You're looking well, Miss Dunn."

Approaching the front desk, Beatrice flashes her invitation to the concierge. "We've come to call on the Baroness Weisshirsch."

"You and half of Manhattan," he says. "Up the stairs and to the left. You can wait in the lounge outside the Baroness's suite, if you can find a seat."

Adelaide rests her elbow on the desk and leans toward the man. "I don't suppose you could find us a way to the front of the line?"

He likes her, always has. He fears her, too, which is an odd, yet marvellous sensation. As a person of consequence in this establishment, he's more used to people being afraid of him. "I wish I could, but I'm not the gatekeeper when it comes to the Baroness. She's brought her own attendants."

"Is Mrs. Stevens in?" Adelaide asks. Her friendship with the hotel's owner is worth more than any bribe she can offer the man.

"She's in London, staying with her daughter, until the New Year."

"Really . . ." Adelaide stares at the man, making it clear she'll not tolerate being lied to.

"Really."

Beatrice gives Adelaide's sleeve a sharp tug. She's spotted the messenger who'd delivered her invitation headed for the stairs. "Let's go," she says.

Adelaide subjects the concierge to another moment of sharp scrutiny, then turns to follow. She'll not be left behind by anyone, least of all Beatrice.

"Excuse me, sir," Beatrice says, as she catches the messenger halfway up the stairs.

"Yes, miss?"

"Remember me?" She holds the envelope up for him to see.

He looks at it and nods. "Right this way."

Walking up the stairs, he leads Beatrice and Adelaide down a long corridor that ends with two facing doors. Opening the door on the left, he gestures to Adelaide. "If you'd be so kind as to wait in here."

The room is filled with people milling about

or sitting in chairs. The noisy throng falls silent when they notice the messenger at the door. Shaking his head at the expectant crowd, he turns to Beatrice and prevents her from following Adelaide into the lounge.

"Where shall I go?" Beatrice asks.

"Come with me."

Just as Adelaide realizes that Beatrice isn't at her side, Judith Dashley descends upon her. As the witches' most ardent admirer, the wealthy woman is responsible for much of their business's success, touting their teas, elixirs and magical gifts to the inner circle of New York society.

"My dear Adelaide!" Judith exclaims, taking her by the arm. "I was hoping I'd see you here. Isn't it just the most exciting turn of events?"

"Just."

Judith steers her to a corner next to a potted palm. "My invitation only arrived late last night. How about yours?"

Adelaide stares in disbelief at the size of the crowd while she attempts to spot Beatrice. "The same."

"Near as I can tell, *everyone* has been invited at the last minute—to a masked ball! Have you ever heard of such a thing in all your life?"

Scanning the room, Adelaide still can't find her friend. "Have you seen Beatrice?"

"How lovely!" Judith exclaims. "So our Miss Dunn has been invited too!"

"But have you seen her?"

"Today?" Judith cranes her neck to look around. "She isn't with you?"

Adelaide fakes a look behind the palm. "She was, and now she isn't. But I'm sure she's here somewhere."

Judith leans close. "They say it took five carriages and two wagons to get the Baroness and her entourage from the docks to the hotel. And that doesn't include all the trappings for the ball, which she had shipped from her Alpine estate."

"Anything for the children."

"The children?"

Adelaide points to her invitation.

DONATIONS WILL BE SOLICITED ON BEHALF *of the* FOUNDATION FOR LOST CHILDREN.

"Why yes, absolutely," Judith says. "That's precisely why I decided to attend on such short notice. Did you know the Baroness has even taken one of our own city's dear orphans under her wing? No wonder Marietta thinks so highly of her."

Adelaide figures it's more likely that the savvy hotelier thinks highly of the increased business the Baroness's ball will bring. "Is it true she won't be here for the big event?"

"Sadly, yes. But she's given the woman carte blanche to do whatever she pleases."

"Interesting," Adelaide says, still finding it a bit hard to believe that Marietta would miss this. *At least the concierge wasn't lying.* Concentrating on who is in the room rather than continuing to search for Beatrice, Adelaide notes a mix of politicians and socialites, old money as well as new. "How do you suppose the Baroness came up with her guest list?"

Judith shrugs. "As far as I can tell there's no rhyme or reason to it, unless of course you consider the number of people here, mixed in among us, who I know have something to hide or hold a grudge against the world."

Adelaide thinks her friend may be on to something. *Charity has never been a single-minded endeavour in this town.* "It's fascinating, to say the least. Perhaps the Baroness is looking to cause a riot?"

"It wouldn't take much with this crowd," Judith says with a laugh.

Normally, Adelaide would press the chatty socialite for details (rumours and gossip come in handy for a fortune teller) but her attention is now fixed on a gentleman who has just entered the room.

In a second her mouth is dry, her palms sweaty, her stomach in turmoil. Adelaide thinks, *It can't be.* Over a decade has passed since she'd last seen the man who'd bought and then taken her innocence when she was just a child. *I tried so hard to forget.* This man is older and greyer than she remembers Mr. Wentworth to be, but he has the same habit of jangling the change in his pocket as he casts around the room for something to excite him. He also carries the same demeanour—arrogant, bored, judgmental, waiting to be impressed. If it's not him, then it's a terrifying likeness. *Surely he won't recognize me, not as I am now.*

She wonders how many others on the Baroness's guest list have committed heinous crimes like Mr. Wentworth committed against her. Could the woman standing just a few feet away be the madam who sold her to him? Could the gentleman next to her be one of the men who bid on her and lost? Is the lady across the room with feathered hat and grating voice, the House of Refuge matron who turned her away as a little girl because she was "too dark, too foreign-looking, too smart-mouthed"?

Not every invitee is a villain. She is sure of that. Judith is kind and good-hearted to a fault. Beatrice is the very picture of innocence and grace.

Which side do I come down on?

One thing she knew: she'd decided long ago to never again be someone's prey. It has left her a little less openhearted and a little more inclined to be cutting and brusque, but she hopes she is never intentionally cruel. *I really must be kinder to Mrs. Stutt.*

Judith touches Adelaide's arm and points to a boisterous clutch of people who've gathered in a nearby corner. "That tall man with the booming laugh over there is a pugilist, I think." Gaily dressed and unconventional in every way, the lively group is far nearer to Adelaide's "kind" than Judith's. "The woman beside him is an actress, and quite a talented one at that. She's been in several *respectable* plays."

Adelaide is amused by her friend's knowledge of the demi-monde, and smiles at her as her eye travels to a little man who is standing on an ottoman in the centre of the group, waving his walking stick in the air while speaking eye-to-eye with his audience. *Mr. Thaddeus Dink.*

As those around him hang on his words, Adelaide edges behind the cover of the potted palm. Unlike the man she suspects to be Mr. Wentworth, Mr. Dink will surely recognize her. This man she doesn't wish to avoid because he wronged her, but because she'd benefited from his kindness then cast him aside once she'd gotten herself a new name and a new life. *Perhaps I am a villain after all.* She shivers at the thought. What kind of game is the Baroness playing at with this ball?

Across the hall in a private reception room, Beatrice is having tea and sweets with the Baroness. Both she and her room are magnificent sights to behold, enveloped in pale blue velvet, with trimmings of silver and gold. The Baroness's white hair is braided in a crown atop her head and kept in place by a small tiara studded with sapphires and pearls. An ermine stole with jet eyes is draped over her left shoulder. Three large wolfhounds sit near her chair, waiting for her command. Each dog wears a jewelled collar—one blue, one yellow, one scarlet.

"More for you?" the Baroness asks, holding a silver teapot, ready to pour.

"I don't know if I should," Beatrice replies. "I've a friend waiting, along with all the others who wish to deliver their replies to you." She feels sleepy and confused, as if dreaming while awake. The chair in which she sits is tufted and soft, its cushions so deep she fears they might swallow her whole.

The Baroness fills her cup. "Adelaide will understand."

Had she mentioned Adelaide by name? *Surely I did.* "Thank you," Beatrice says, sipping her tea. "You're very kind."

"Kindness begets kindness."

The hound in blue lays its head at Beatrice's feet. Reaching down, she strokes the dog's soft fur.

"He likes you," the Baroness says.

Beatrice smiles.

"Tell me, Miss Dunn, is it true that you can hear spirits?"

Taken aback, Beatrice wonders if Marietta Stevens told the Baroness about her ability. Perhaps that's why she's been invited to the ball. "Yes," she cautiously admits.

"What a boon," the woman says. "You must find it quite useful."

"Sometimes." Just when Beatrice thinks her host is about to inquire after her services, the Baroness slides a plate of sweets in front of her instead.

"Gingerbread, springerle, fairy cake, or some *Engelszopf*?"

As the girl reaches for a slice of almond-sprinkled sweet loaf, a chorus of strange voices and gentle noises titter around her—whispers, laughter, birdsong, rainfall, the tinkling of bells. It's unsettling and enchanting all at once, unlike anything (human or spirit) she's ever heard. *Where is it coming from? Does the Baroness hear it?*

At a snap of the Baroness's fingers, the voices fall silent and a young woman appears in the doorway of an adjoining room. Slight and delicate, with a halo of dark curls and striking blue eyes, she bows to her mistress and then to Beatrice.

"Fetch Miss Dunn's mask," the Baroness commands.

With a nod, the girl disappears, and returns with a box clad in silver foil and gold ribbon. She hands it to Beatrice and takes her leave.

Tugging at the bow, Beatrice opens the package and stares at what's inside, aware that the Baroness is watching her closely.

"It's beautiful," Beatrice says as she lifts the mask from the box and admires every inch of it, inside and out. Fashioned from silk, leather, fur, feathers and gemstones, it is the perfect likeness of a fox. The dizzy confusion she's been feeling fades as she holds the mask in front of her face and looks through the fox's eyes at the Baroness.

"It suits you," the woman says. "It brings out your cunning, and cleverness."

Gently returning the mask to the box, Beatrice pauses once more to admire it before replacing the box's lid. "I'll take good care of it, I promise."

Licking a dusting of sugar from the tip of one finger, the Baroness slyly grins at her. "See that you do."

Baroness Weisshirsch's Engelszopf
(angel braid)

This traditional German sweet bread is made during the winter holiday season and most often served with coffee, tea or hot chocolate at brunch. Some say that such braided breads were first made to pay homage to the ancient custom of women offering their braids of hair to the goddess Perchta, also known as Berchta or Holle.

Ingredients:

1/3 cup golden raisins
5 tablespoons of kirschwasser (cherry brandy)

1/2 cup butter
1/2 cup heavy cream
1/2 cup sour cream
1/3 cup brown sugar
3 tablespoons honey
2 1/4 teaspoons active dry yeast (1 package)

continued...

1/3 cup sliced almonds
1/3 cup candied orange peel, diced
3 1/2–4 cups flour
2 eggs

Topping:
1 egg
2 tablespoons milk
1/4 cup slivered almonds

Method:

Soak raisins in brandy for 20 minutes.

In a saucepan, melt butter on low heat, then add
heavy cream, sour cream, brown sugar and honey.
Gently stir until ingredients are combined, then
bring to a warm temperature (but not to a boil).
Remove from heat and stir in yeast. Set aside for 15
minutes (mixture should start to bubble as the yeast
becomes active).

Drain raisins and combine with 1/3 cup sliced
almonds and orange peel. Toss mixture with a bit of
flour. (This will keep the fruit from sticking
together.) Set aside.

In a large mixing bowl, beat two eggs. Add the cream mixture to the eggs a little at a time until fully combined. Stir one cup of flour into the mixture, followed by the fruits and nuts. Continue to add flour until the mixture is formed into a soft dough. Turn out onto a floured surface and knead until smooth. Return to a bowl and cover with a warm, moist towel. Let rise for one hour.

Return the dough to a floured surface and knead out any air bubbles. Separate the dough into three equal pieces and roll each piece into a length about twelve inches long. Braid the three lengths together to form a loaf. Let rise in a warm, draft-free spot for 45 minutes.

To prepare the loaf for baking, beat one egg yolk together with milk and then brush over the braided loaf. Sprinkle with sliced almonds.

Bake in a pre-heated oven at 350°F for 30–40 minutes, or until the loaf is golden brown and makes a hollow sound when you tap it with your finger.

Adelaide is alone in her room at the end of the day, staring at the box that contains her mask. Her meeting with the Baroness had been far shorter than Beatrice's. There'd been no small talk or wonder; no cookies and tea.

"Why do you wish to attend my ball?" the elegant woman had asked, like a queen on a throne, petting one of her loyal hounds.

Adelaide had chosen to answer the Baroness's question with one of her own. "Why did you invite me?" She refused to grovel for anyone's approval.

The Baroness had returned Adelaide's impertinence with a laugh. "I admire a woman who speaks her mind. This world could certainly do with more honesty. Wouldn't you agree?"

"Wholeheartedly."

Neither woman had pressed the other any further.

The mask the Baroness had presented to Adelaide was that of a moth, made from peacock feathers and iridescent green satin, fitted with a glimmering glass eye on the same side as the one she herself had lost. There'd been no explanation as to how the woman had known about her disfigurement or that long ago her father had sworn that a magical pear tree had bid him to name her Moth. Adelaide had been so taken aback, she hadn't bothered to ask for one. It was rare for her to encounter someone as well informed about the denizens of New York as the Baroness was, especially a stranger.

Picking up the exquisite object, Adelaide now wonders if there's something more behind the mask's design. The longer she examines the elegant creation, the more she thinks it likely that the Baroness is sending her a message: *I know who you are.*

She hopes the ball is not a trap. Seeing both Mr. Wentworth and Mr. Dink among the eager invitees had thrown her. Does the Baroness know the whole of her sordid past? Does she plan to use it against her? Based on the number of people with guilty secrets that'd been present in the room, it seemed a strong possibility. Perhaps it wasn't meant to be a New Year's celebration, but a night for settling scores.

She'd managed to exit the hotel without either man recognizing her, but her escape had left her feeling helpless rather than relieved. Keeping that part of her life separate from the person she'd become had seemed the right thing to do, until now. Other than Eleanor, no one in the city knows her completely, warts and all. It occurs to her that leaving the past so thoroughly behind has made her quite lonely, even in the company of the man she loves.

What would her dear Dr. Brody say if he found out about her past? Would he still want to marry her? He knows she comes from low beginnings, but she's told him little else, and thankfully, he hasn't pressed. He understands she's not a perfect rose.

But to tell him she worked as a hustler in Mr. Dink's sideshow was hard for her to contemplate. To tell him she'd sold her virtue when she was an orphan child trying to survive on the streets of New York seems impossible. He'd been wonderfully sincere and kind with her. Even his proposal had been offered with patience and care. "I ask you this, without expecting an immediate answer. I only hope that you'll have one for me when I return." If she puts him off when he comes home, will he ever ask again?

"You must tell him everything," Eleanor had advised. "There should be no secrets between man and wife."

Pacing the floor, Adelaide considers her choices.

She takes a penny from her pocket and flips it into the air with her thumb. *Heads, yes. Tails, no.* It falls in a crack between the floorboards and disappears. She has to laugh. *Why can't things ever be easy for me?*

Lifting a book from her desk she closes her eyes, lets it fall open, then places her finger in the middle of a page, hoping the word she's landed on will give her some direction. Opening her eyes she lifts her finger and discovers the word is "or."

What have I got to offer him? I'm no one. Worse, I'm a fraud.

Shuffling the deck of fortune-telling cards she uses to assist the women of New York in finding their destinies, she pulls a single card and turns it over. A cloaked figure stands on a precipice, staring into a great chasm. CONTEMPLATION.

Maybe I won't go to the ball.

Maybe I'll say no to love.

Or maybe I'll say yes to everything.

Beatrice is sequestered in her room down the hall, recording her thoughts on the day in her book of observations.

What a magnificent woman the Baroness is! Just as wise as she is generous. I was so impressed by her that I find I can't recall all she said. I hope I'll get to speak with her again.

Lifting her mask from its box, she holds it to her face and ties the ribbons around her head. Gazing at herself in the mirror she whispers, "You vixen." Perdu watches intently from atop one of the posts of her bed. When Beatrice turns to him and curtsies, he whistles and coos.

A sudden noise at the window startles them both—a stray cat clawing and crying at the sill.

Beatrice opens the sash and greets it with a friendly "hello," forgetting she still wears the face of a fox.

The startled calico hisses and growls.

Perdu responds in kind.

"Come now, you two," Beatrice scolds, untying the ribbons and setting the mask aside. "Can't we be friends?"

This isn't the first time the cat has visited. It's been coming to the window every night for the past month.

"Surely this time you'll come inside," Beatrice coaxes. "Even to shake the snow off your paws?"

The cat refuses, as she always does.

"Bad kit-ty," Perdu croaks, as *he* always does.

Pulling apart a small hunk of boiled beef she'd taken from the pantry for the pair, Beatrice sits on the window ledge and feeds both cat and bird. "One for you," she tells Perdu, who's now on the verge of sitting in her lap. "And one for you," she says to the cat, who's poised and cautious just outside the window.

She hopes eventually to earn the feline's trust. She adores Perdu but misses having a warm companion curled at the end of her bed as she sleeps. Her dog Cleo had disappeared one rainy evening in the autumn and had never come back. The hound had taken to chasing rats drawn to the refuse Mrs. Stutt threw off the back stoop, and all anyone could think was that the determined animal had chased one of the vermin too far and couldn't find its way back home. Beatrice had been crushed, repeatedly wondering out loud if there was anything she could have done to prevent the dog's disappearance. Eleanor had tried to comfort her: "Short of keeping it tethered to your side, I doubt you could have stopped it. When a dog follows its nose, trouble follows it." Adelaide had been more blunt. "Maybe the pup was just bored."

Over time, Beatrice had come to see Adelaide's point of view. In the year that'd passed since she'd come to live with the two witches, she's gone from feeling protected and safe and valued for her unique qualities to feeling watched and confined. *Tethered, indeed.* She knows how it feels to be at the end of a short leash.

Adelaide, of course (who fiercely relishes her own freedom), has never been one to make her feel that way, but after her abduction by the vile minister—a horrible episode Beatrice tries not to think about—Eleanor swiftly hemmed her in, constantly hovering over her, questioning her every move, and refusing to let her to try magic on her own.

She wishes her relationship with the wise woman could be more like the one she's created with Dr. Brody. Her work with him on understanding the ways of the dead has been steady and satisfying—a source of confidence and pride. They've solved several ghostly mysteries in Manhattan and the surrounding boroughs—some real, some imagined, some contrived. He often sets aside his experience and scholarship to ask her for advice. He freely gives her praise and respect, and more importantly, responsibility. If only Eleanor would do the same.

She'd thought the aim of being Eleanor's apprentice was to help her find her way to her powers as a witch, but now she's wondering if maybe she'd thought wrong. The more she tries to take initiative, the more Eleanor resists, so she's resorted to keeping things to herself, not just her dreams of the Stranger, but the spells and incantations she attempts in secret. *How will I learn to trust my instincts if I'm never allowed to follow them?*

The cat, noting Beatrice's distraction, bites the ribbon at the end of the girl's long braid. Tugging it loose, the stray runs off with it.

"Come back!" Beatrice calls, too late.

Hopping to the sill, Perdu squawks his disapproval. "Baaaad kit-ty."

"Some witch I am." Beatrice says. "I can't even tame a hungry cat."

My Dearest Eleanor,

I am comfortably settled in the City of Light and missing you beyond belief. While I'm eager to begin my studies at the Academie, I do wish that you were here. I know six months is not a lifetime, but each day is an eon without you by my side. Won't you please come stay with me a while? I need the aid of your native tongue. I am far more confident with ink, press, paint and brush than I am with the language of love. Beatrice must be ready by now to sit at the helm of the Hermitage. Let her pilot the ship so that you may set sail to my arms.

Yours,

Georgina

Eleanor is tucked away in her room, thinking on her own condition. Kissing an inky smudge in the left corner of the page, she longs for her lover's touch. She misses Georgina's voice too, and the quick ease of her smile.

I would leave if I could.

I would fly to your side . . .

Georgina Davis had stolen Eleanor's heart almost as unexpectedly as she'd entered her life. All ink and broken pencils, honesty and forthrightness, this woman who made her living illustrating the highs and lows of New York life for the newspapers, was now someone Eleanor didn't wish to live without. Georgina's kindness had seen her through the terrible days when Beatrice was missing. Her love and affection had helped her find her way back to herself.

Folding the letter, Eleanor tucks it in her pocket. She plans to reread it many times before the night is over, but she needs something to soothe her sadness and heal her heart first. Tea will have to do.

She tightens her robe about her and goes downstairs. As she enters the kitchen, she's met with a strange sight. Mrs. Stutt is standing before a steaming teapot, eyes closed, arms outstretched, hands to Heaven in the posture of magic, of prayer. She is half-singing, half-chanting in a haunting language Eleanor has never heard.

When she falls silent at last, Eleanor gently says, "Mrs. Stutt?"

The housekeeper gives a start. "Miss St. Clair, I didn't see you there." Wiping her hands on her apron, she glances at the china teapot. "I was just making some tea for Miss Dunn."

"What kind?" Eleanor asks. "I might like some for myself."

"Just an old family recipe, a winter tonic of sorts."

Eleanor sniffs the air. *Elderflower—to clear the lungs, cool the blood, and quell one's fears.* "Is Beatrice unwell?"

The steam escaping the spout of the pot now swirls and gathers, taking on the shape of an unearthly spectre. *"Blicket auf!"* the spirit commands. As Mrs. Stutt opens her mouth in shock, it slithers between her parted lips.

"Behold!" the housekeeper says, in a voice not her own. Reaching into her pocket, she takes the lead from Beatrice's divination and holds it up against the light of the fire.

Eleanor watches in fear as a demon's shadow spreads and grows upon the wall and opens its hungry maw.

"What have you done?" she cries, snatching the object from the woman's hand.

"He is coming for her. He'll arrive before the dead days are done." Grasping for Eleanor, Mrs. Stutt collapses and slumps to the floor.

"Mrs. Stutt." Eleanor cradles the woman in her arms, attempting to revive her. "Mrs. Stutt . . ."

I would leave if I could.

I would fly to your side . . .

But Beatrice needs me.

Mr. Gideon Palsham sits in his parlour in front of a roaring fire. Every so often he spits whiskey between his teeth at the flames. He likes to make things dance and leap.

A soft thud sounds at the window behind him, followed by the loud, steady purr of a cat. He'd left the window open, anticipating her return. He smiles when the feline's purring changes to footfalls at his back and her breathing assumes the cadence of human form. "Miss Miles, I'm so glad you've come home."

A naked, lithe, Sophie Miles comes to him and sits in his lap, clutching Beatrice's hair ribbon between her teeth.

Palsham had plucked her from the lunatic asylum on Blackwell's Island after he'd discovered that she'd been the person responsible for Adelaide Thom's disfigurement. They'd quickly formed a pact: she is to do his bidding (in whatever manner he wishes) and he'll refrain from killing her (for the time being). He may have also promised her immortality, but that doesn't really matter much right now.

Sophie runs Beatrice's hair ribbon between her

teeth, then drapes it around her master's neck. "Mr. Palshammmm," she says, rubbing her cheek against his beard and sinking her nails into his arm.

He appreciates the pain. "Does this mean you went inside her room?"

She shakes her head. "I don't like the bird."

Palsham laughs. "Scaredy cat."

"You're mean," Sophie complains. "Just like the raven."

Palsham grins and runs his tongue along the edge of his teeth. "I know I am." Taking the young woman's chin in his hand, he holds it steady and stares into her eyes. He can see Beatrice in her room, sitting at the window, wearing her fox mask. "She's going to the ball," he says, pleased.

Sophie writhes against him, hungry for affection.

Palsham shifts in his seat, shrugs her off. "Be gone."

As the young woman passes through the fire-light, she resumes the form of her imprisonment. With a hiss she scampers out of the room and down the hall.

Winding Beatrice's ribbon around his finger, Palsham can barely control his excitement. And why should he? He's been working hard for the moment when the girl will be delivered to him. He's followed her for months, watching her from the shadows, always from a distance, waiting for his chance. *Soon she'll be mine.*

For the longest time, he'd had plans to destroy her, just as he'd done away with countless other witches throughout the ages. But she was singular, powerful, different. His plan to have that incompetent preacher end her had gone horribly wrong, and he'd only had himself to blame. Now the places where she lives and works are fortresses of vexation, heavily guarded by witchcraft he can't overcome. *One should never send a man to do a demon's work.*

As bothersome as that failure had been, it'd given him time to see how truly spectacular the girl was meant to become. One evening, while sucking the marrow from her dead dog's bones he'd seen the light. He'd come to realize that destroying her wasn't the thing that would be of greatest benefit to him, but rather possessing her. Now it was a race to catch her while her power was ascending, her mind still supple and longing to learn, eager and foolish enough for magic that she would agree to his terms. The longer he waits, the greater the chance that she and the other witches she lives with will seek to thwart his plan. *The time is now.*

Letting the ribbon go, he watches it spiral and curl to the floor. Oh, how he loves to make things dance.

Mrs. Stutt's
Elderflower Syrup

The elder tree has long been revered as a plant with
both medicinal properties and magical qualities.
Various European cultures associated it with the
Elder Mother, or Holle, or the White Lady, claiming
that the tree was her dwelling place and its roots, the
entrance to the underworld. Planting an elder tree
near a home was believed to bring blessings to the
house's occupants. Falling asleep under an elder tree
in full bloom was said to lead to supernatural visions.
Harvesting flowers or berries from the sacred plant
without giving proper thanks to the goddess would
surely bring bad luck. Some even referred to the
plant as "the witch's tree" because its flowers and
fruit were favoured among female healers who knew
of the plant's curative effects on respiratory illnesses,
fevers and anxious hearts.

This lovely golden syrup is made in spring when the elder trees are in bloom, but its light, delicate flavour will surely brighten even the coldest of winter nights.

Ingredients:

15–20 elderflower umbels
6 cups water
6 cups sugar
1 teaspoon citric acid
2 lemons

Method:

Harvest elderflowers while in full bloom but before they begin to turn brown and fade. If you're gathering them in the wild, make certain they're plants that yield blue-purple berries (*Sambucus canadensis* or *Sambucus nigra*) rather than red. Snip the entire umbel from the plant with scissors and use a cloth bag or basket, not plastic, for collecting them to prevent the flowers from sweating and wilting.

Clean the umbels of debris and insects, then trim the individual blossoms from their stems. Put the blossoms in a large bowl and set aside.

Combine the sugar and water in a pot; set on stove over medium-high heat and stir until sugar is dissolved. Bring to a boil then reduce heat and keep at a low boil for five minutes. Remove from heat and stir in citric acid.

Cut the lemons into slices and put in bowl with elderflowers. Pour syrup mixture over the flowers and lemons and stir gently. Cover the bowl and store in a cool, dry place for 48 hours. Stir once per day.

After 48 hours, strain the syrup through a sieve lined with cheesecloth into a clean pot. Bring the syrup to a boil, then pour into canning jars and screw on lids. Place jars in a boiling water bath for 10 minutes to sterilize.

The syrup should keep for up to a year. Opened jars should be refrigerated.

Elderflower syrup is a wonderful addition to tea, sparkling water, lemonade, and cocktails. It can be used on its own over waffles, fresh fruit, pavlova, or ice cream; or used to flavour whipped cream, sponge cake or frosting.

DECEMBER 31

The day of the ball has arrived. All along
Fifth Avenue, eager guests rush from dress-
maker to haberdasher to shoemaker to hair-
dresser in anticipation of the evening's festivities.
Those without an invitation attempt to curry
favour with the Baroness, sending wildly generous
donations along with note after note to the hotel
believing there's still time to win her over.

One leading lady of Gotham, unaccustomed
to exclusion, sends ten baskets of roses, five pounds
of chocolate and a jewelled brooch from Tiffany &
Co. to the Baroness's suite, all before eight in the
morning.

I would be honoured . . .
I would be forever grateful . . .
I'll be indebted to you always . . .

While enjoying a breakfast of coffee, fried mushrooms, toast and sausages, the Baroness thumbs through the towering stack of missives on her desk. She spins the brooch between her fingers, amused, yet unmoved. She'd made her list ages ago and checked it several times over. There's no room for last-minute stragglers, no matter how exquisite their bribery.

One floor below, Adelaide and Beatrice are ensconced in a suite that belongs to Judith Dashley. The wealthy matron has a palatial mansion further uptown, but keeps rooms at the hotel for special occasions and emergencies. She considers the preparations for the ball to be both.

Due to the meagre amount of time the women have been given to ready themselves for the masquerade, Judith has insisted she supply the witches with gowns from her vast collection. "The fit won't be perfect, mind you, but with a few strategically placed pins and the ballroom's dim lighting, you'll both look smashing." Pointing to a third dress draped across a nearby chaise, she adds, "There's one for Eleanor, in case she changes her mind. Be sure to take it with you."

"She won't change her mind," Adelaide says.

"But that's very kind of you," Beatrice interjects. Truth be told, she's somewhat glad Eleanor's not going. She's certain the woman would insist on trailing after her the entire time.

The trio settles down for morning tea before getting on with the rest of their day.

Judith pours first for Adelaide, then Beatrice, and then for herself. "The hotel staff has been scurrying about day and night to do the Baroness's bidding. I tried to steal a peek at the preparations, but the ballroom is under lock and key. No guests are allowed in until tonight, and the maids have been sworn to secrecy. I stood in the hallway outside the room for over an hour, hoping I might overhear something."

"And did you?" Beatrice asks, stirring sugar into her tea.

"Not a peep," Judith admits. "I'm starting to think the work's being done by elves in the middle of the night."

Adelaide grins as she lifts her cup from its saucer. "Maybe the Baroness brought them with her, along with everything else."

Beatrice rolls her eyes. Adelaide is always so flippant. "I can't wait for tonight. I find it all very exciting."

Judith asks, tentatively, "I don't suppose you'd be willing to call on the hotel's resident spirits for their thoughts on the matter? The suspense is killing me."

Beatrice shakes her head. "As dear as you are to me, Judith, I must decline. I prefer to be surprised."

This was something of a lie. On her way to Judith's suite, she'd slipped away from Adelaide and into a linen closet to corner the spirit of a charwoman and ask her what she knew about the ball. The ghostly maid had refused to answer.

"And none of the rest of us will tell you neither, so don't go asking around." Beatrice couldn't tell if the spectre was afraid of the Baroness or simply in her thrall like everyone else clearly seemed to be.

As the noon bells toll from the churches near Madison Square, a hush falls over the hotel. The quiet seeps out of the building to the surrounding sidewalks and across the avenue to the park. Birds stop their singing. Passersby cease their talk.

The Baroness stands from her desk and turns to her attendant. "The time has come."

The angel-faced girl dutifully fetches the last two boxes and tucks them under her arms.

Donning a fur-lined cloak, the Baroness leads the girl out of the hotel and into the street.

Passersby whisper in wonder. The birds resume their songs.

Unsettled by the warning delivered through Mrs. Stutt, Eleanor has spent the morning casting renewed protection spells on the witches' home and shop—reciting prayers and incantations as she blesses every room with incense and sprinkles every doorway with salt.

The housekeeper had quickly recovered from her strange episode in the kitchen but claimed she could not remember what had happened. Eleanor could not forget.

"Think what you like," the old housekeeper had said. "But I'm sure it's just a case of the nerves. You know how unreliable women get when they grow old. Bones talk, the mind wanders, ears grow eyes. My dear grandmother used to babble for hours about the trolls that danced in the woods behind the barn and the night they led the evil Prince Georg to be taken up by the Wild Hunt. The minute I start talking about gnomes playing ninepins in the cellar, ship me back to the Schwarzwald so they can feed me to the wild boars."

"I'll do no such thing," Eleanor had chided. "You're needed here." She only wished that whatever had moved through Mrs. Stutt (be it a case of the nerves or a godforsaken spirit) had mentioned the how, where and when of the demon's scheming.

She'd wanted to tell Beatrice of the apparition in the shadows, to warn her at the very least, but the girl had been out the door with Adelaide before breakfast. Now, the more she thinks on things, the more she's inclined to advise her apprentice that she shouldn't leave the house again until further notice. That, of course, would include not going to the ball. She knows Beatrice will take it badly, but how else can she keep the girl safe?

Pulling her grimoire off the shelf, she begins to search for answers. "Dear Maman," she whispers to the air, "show me the way."

Before she can lift the book's cover, Mrs. Stutt comes to interrupt her. "There's a visitor for you. The Baroness Weisshirsch."

Eleanor follows the housekeeper to the door and finds the imposing woman standing on the stoop with a young girl at her side. Perdu is guarding the threshold.

The Baroness is a stranger to Eleanor, but the child is quite familiar to her. She's the waif that'd led her and Adelaide to the church where Beatrice had been held prisoner. She hadn't seen the girl since. *Why on earth are they together?* Still, no matter how the pair had crossed paths, she's glad to see the child looking so well and cared for.

"Baroness Weisshirsch," she says, "do come in." Smiling at the girl, she gestures for her to do the same.

"Thank you, Miss St. Clair," the Baroness says, escorting her charge into the foyer. Perdu sidles up to the pair and chortles a soft "hello." His behaviour startles his mistress. As a rule, her familiar doesn't talk to strangers. (With the occasional exception for witches and ghosts.)

"To what do I owe the pleasure?" Eleanor asks, somewhat impatiently. She's anxious to head to the hotel to retrieve Beatrice sooner rather than later.

Taking the box that rests under the girl's right arm, the Baroness presents it to Eleanor. "I've brought your mask for the ball."

Eleanor takes the package and sets it on a small table against the wall. "It's kind of you to go to the trouble, but I never accepted your invitation to the masquerade because I don't intend on going."

"Are you certain?" the woman asks. "I've a perfect record when it comes to attendance. In all my years of experience, no one has ever declined my invitation."

"Is that so?" Eleanor says, pointing to the box that remains tucked under the orphan's left arm.

The Baroness calmly smiles. "Mr. Palsham *will* be attending."

"Mr. Gideon Palsham?" Eleanor feels a chill as she remembers Beatrice's account of crossing paths with him in the park. The girl had suffered more nightmares from his brief touch than from the whole of the torture put upon her by Reverend Townsend.

"You know him, then?"

"He has a certain reputation."

"He is quite the devil," the Baroness says.

Wings flapping, chest puffed, Perdu begins to hiss and squawk.

"Hush!" Eleanor says, attempting to quiet the bird's outrage.

Reaching into the pocket of her cloak, the Baroness pulls out a small parcel wrapped in red silk. Untying the bundle, she bends low and holds the contents out to the bird. "Come have a treat," she coaxes. "So you'll feel like yourself again."

Eleanor watches in amazement as her familiar obeys the woman's command. The bird turns quiet and docile the instant he swallows the first morsel from her hand.

"*Engelszopf*," the Baroness says. "The sweetest delight in all of Germany. I'll send you the recipe." Straightening herself up she declares, "And now I'd best be going. I'm not one for unfinished business."

Placing a hand on the box that contains the mask, Eleanor says, "Neither am I."

5

In the corners of the world where ancient forests shelter mystical creatures, and sacred springs hold the voices of nymphs, wise women pause Between the Years to honour the one who rules them all, the Queen of Witches.

Some call her the Mistress of Yule, others call her Frau Perchta, or Holle, or Bertha, or Bright One, or the Lady of the Dead. Her name does not matter half so much as her gifts, for she alone has the power to lead the Wild Hunt.

Eleanor kisses the tip of her finger and touches it to her grimoire. "For luck."

Beatrice and Adelaide do the same. "For luck."

"For luck."

The three witches are standing in the cupola that sits atop Dr. Brody's house. It was built for observing the night sky, but tonight, the witches are there to observe an ancient rite.

Leave your wheel and spindle idle. Don your cloak and cover your face. Steal to rooftop or sacred grove bearing offerings for the Mistress. Burn fires of holly and oak. Bring libations of honey and the fruits of the wood to show your faith.

With a small bowl in hand, Eleanor casts a mixture of flaxseed, oats and holly berries to the wind. "Dear Queen, we thank you for the bounty in our lives."

Adelaide pours elderberry wine from a silver goblet onto the roof's slate shingles. "Dear Queen, we praise you for being generous and wise."

Striking a match against the metal railing of the cupola, Beatrice sets the contents of a brass censer on fire. A feathery nest of herbs, wood shavings and three strips of paper catch light as she feeds the flames with her breath. Each piece of paper contains a wish.

May the past be resolved.

May evil be met with justice.

May the way be made clear.

As the smoke rises, Beatrice says, "We call on you, O Queen, to come to our aid."

She comes in the nights of Rauhnächt to cleanse the earth of secrets, sorrows, lies, and demons. Great blessings come to those who assist her with her work, but beware the consequences. Many a witch has been taken up in her riotous frenzy and has been swept away in a journey through both heaven and underworld. Petition her at your peril.

Once the three women are finished and back in the house proper, they dress for the ball and prepare for battle.

Hair is combed and pinned, corset laces tightened. Adelaide stows a sharp, thin blade in a leather sheath and buckles it to her leg. Eleanor fastens an amulet of protection around Beatrice's neck, then dresses herself in the gown Judith had set aside for her "just in case."

"You look radiant," Adelaide tells her. "The gown suits you perfectly."

The minute the Baroness had spoken of Mr. Palsham, Eleanor had decided to join her sister witches at the masquerade. Her desire to watch over Beatrice became all the more keen when she'd opened the box that'd contained her mask. Along with the magnificent feathered likeness of a great-horned owl, had been a note that read: *J'ai vu le loup.* They were the same words her mother had once sent to her from beyond the grave to warn her that Beatrice was in danger. *I saw the wolf.*

Eleanor was now convinced that the Baroness was far more than a woman of social consequence. At the very least, she was a witch, and quite possibly something more. If that was the case, then it followed that Mr. Palsham could well be the demon Mrs. Stutt had shown her in the shadows on the wall. The signs all pointed to something much larger than anything she'd ever encountered—to magic far beyond the physical world. She only hopes the instructions in the pages of her grimoire will deliver as promised. If all that she is thinking is true, then it will take the Queen of Witches to see them through.

"Are you certain you wish to go through with this?" she asks her friends. She'd told them all she knew of Mr. Palsham, and the possible danger in her plan, but she needs to hear them say once more they're willing to take the risk. "I can't promise there won't be dire consequences."

Beatrice reaches for Eleanor's hand. "Whatever happens, we're in this together."

Taking a flask from her reticule, Adelaide unscrews the lid and takes a sip. "Schnapps," she says, "for courage, and catching demons."

Beatrice takes the flask in hand, lifts it in a toast. "To catching demons."

Eleanor takes her own small sip then walks to the door to pour a splash of liquor on the stoop. *One last offering can't hurt.* "To catching demons."

The witches arrive at the hotel to find the ball-room has been transformed into an enchanting Alpine wood. Spruce, pine and holly boughs, decked with colourful lanterns, line the walls. The Baroness's footmen stand at attention by the door with long boar spears in hand. A brook trickles down a craggy waterfall as high as the ceiling and runs through the middle of the room. A wooden footbridge arches across the stream, leading to a stone well that bears the sign: *Please leave donations here.* At the opposite end of the room is an enormous fireplace with a large copper cauldron suspended above it. Nearby, the punch master stands at the ready, his crystal bowl filled to the brim. Two large tables on either side of him are dressed with pine boughs and laden with sugared fruit and confections envel-oped in marzipan. Lively music fills the air as the crowd of masked guests flies across the dance floor, each transformed into a woodland creature, real and imagined. Badger, mink, squirrel, bear, hawk, deer, snake, wolf, toad. Gnome, elf, boar, porcupine, beaver, dragonfly, ladybird, katydid, lark, wren, dryad. Lynx, troll, pheasant, hag, hare, cardinal, waxwing, snail, trout.

Beatrice can't stop staring at a peculiar instrument set among the musicians in the orchestra. Nestled between accordion and fiddles, horns and hurdy-gurdy, is a series of glass bowls set on their sides in two long rows, made to spin by a treadle. A woman dressed in a long white gown is playing the instrument by running her fingers along the rims of each glass in quick succession. Every so often, she dips her fingertips in a tray of water and then resumes her performance. The sound the thing makes reminds Beatrice of the voices she'd heard in the Baroness's suite.

"It's a glass harmonica," a cheerful goldfinch chirps in Beatrice's ear. Judith Dashley has made her way to the girl. They'd broken with tradition and chosen to share their identities with each other in advance of the ball. "Alden has one of those diabolical things in the cellar of our house in Tarrytown. He sneaks downstairs and plays it in the middle of the night to put a fright in me. Good thing he's off to Washington with Dr. Brody and the rest of his fellow philosophers or he'd be trying to buy this one for the house on Marble Row."

Beatrice turns to Adelaide, in her glittering disguise. "Wouldn't Dr. Brody love one?"

"Yes," Adelaide replies. "I'm sure he would." She spots a jaunty badger in top hat and tails across the room, and her stomach flutters. Thaddeus Dink is unmistakable, even at a masquerade. *At least there's no sign of Mr. Wentworth,* she thinks, and hopes it will stay that way. Perhaps her mind had been playing tricks on her in the Baroness's waiting lounge the other day.

"Eleanor St. Clair?" Judith asks, recognizing her own gown before she does the stately figure of the witch. "How wonderful that you changed your mind!"

Eleanor smiles and nods as she scans the room for signs of trouble.

Adelaide leans close and says, "I'll know him if I see him."

As the orchestra plays a seductive waltz, Judith points to a young man advancing toward Beatrice. "I see a dashing gentleman in your future."

He is tall and stately, with a sleek feathered raven's mask and a long black braid down his back. A small gold hoop glints in his ear. He stops a moment to smooth his lapels, straighten his tie and pick a stray piece of lint from the sleeve of his coat. His suit is so new it shines. Beatrice recognizes him in an instant. Her Stranger. With all of Eleanor's talk of demons and goddesses, she'd almost forgotten the chestnut's promise.

As the young man bows to her and then extends his hand, she bites her tongue for fear of saying, *It's you.* Thrilled by his presence, she puts her hand in his.

"May I have this dance?" he asks. His voice is as familiar to her as her own.

Judith whispers to Adelaide, "What a perfect pair they make."

Adelaide stares hard at the young man. He looks nothing like the trollish gent who'd accosted Beatrice last year in the park.

"Do you know him?" Eleanor whispers to Judith.

"I don't think so. But his bearing is quite regal, don't you think? Perhaps he's here with the Baroness."

Beatrice nods at the man, and he whisks her away to the dance floor. There are hundreds of questions she could ask the Stranger but, transfixed by his dark shining eyes, she stays silent as he leads her in dance after dance. If she's dreaming, she doesn't wish to wake.

While Beatrice falls under the Stranger's spell, Eleanor keeps her eyes on the pair. She could swear she's seen the young man somewhere before.

Adelaide gathers her courage and goes in search of refreshment and Mr. Dink. She's resolved to speak to him before he recognizes her. It's a night for exorcising demons, after all.

"Excuse me, sir," she says, as she approaches the merry little gentleman, who is hovering near the punch bowl. Taking a deep breath she thinks, *Now or never.*

"No excuse required," he replies, tipping his hat.

"Spare a minute for an old friend?" Adelaide asks.

Mr. Dink raises his mask and winks. "You don't look so old to me, dear Moth. Then taking Adelaide's hand in his, he warmly kisses it. "You may have chosen to forget me, but I will never forget you."

His words move her heart in ways she hadn't expected. She wishes to raise her own mask, so he will see the burned side of her face, the lost eye, but this is enough for now, she decides.

"Tell me, dear girl, how are you?"

"I'm well."

"And happy?"

She blushes and stammers. "A—actually, yes."

"Someone's won my little Moth's heart! How tremendous."

"I hope so. At least I think it is."

"Why wouldn't it be?"

Adelaide feels as if she's a child again, struggling to find a safe place to land. If she's to give Dr. Brody her heart, completely and without any secrets, she needs to know what Mr. Dink had seen in her all those years ago. If he could love her when she was at her lowest, then perhaps she wasn't as hopeless as she thought. "Why did you take me in after I was ruined? What made you think I was worth caring for?"

Bringing her hand to his cheek, he regards her long and steadily, before he replies. "My life was made brighter the minute you walked into it," he says. "I adored you from the start. I couldn't imagine not caring for you."

Tearful, Adelaide smiles. They are the same words she's heard time and again from her beloved Dr. Brody. "I'm sorry I haven't been to see you since my circumstances changed. I had some trouble, but it's over now, I hope."

"I'm glad to hear it," Mr. Dink replies. "Come see me, my lovely Moth. And you'd better bring that man of yours along so I can judge if he's good enough for you."

"I will. I promise."

Eleanor checks the watch that dangles from her chatelaine. It reads quarter to twelve. *Where has the time gone?* Beatrice has been dancing in plain sight the entire time, and Mr. Palsham, demon or not, hasn't come forth. Could she have misinterpreted the signs? Soon the clocks will strike midnight, the revellers will ring in the New Year, and the ball will be over. *What then?*

A woman dressed in rags and wearing the mask of a frightful hag appears at her side. "Where is she?" she croaks.

"Pardon?" Eleanor asks.

The woman points a crooked finger at the dance floor. "The fox is gone."

Eleanor pushes her way through the twirling dancers, frantically searching for Beatrice.

"Wait," Beatrice calls as she runs out the ballroom doors after the Stranger. The young man had broken free from her embrace without explanation and vanished.

As she runs down a long corridor, she sees him slip into a conservatory made of glass. Lit by a series of magnificent chandeliers, each pane in the walls and ceiling shimmers like a thousand glowing stars.

Her pursuit stops short when she finds the Stranger standing face to face with Mr. Palsham. Shrinking back against the door, she hides behind a large marble statue of a Grecian water bearer. She trembles as she watches the two men, hardly believing they are in the same room: the man of her dreams and the man of her nightmares. She was supposed to have drawn the demon into the witches' trap, not the other way around. *How could I have been so stupid?* Her blood runs cold when she realizes the young man is holding a dagger.

"Malphas!" the Stranger shouts, circling her tormentor. "I command you to be gone!"

In an instant Mr. Palsham is transformed, his fingers turned to claws, his suit to rags, his face fanged and snarling. The deep scars around his lips glisten in the gaslight. The smell of sulphur and rotting flesh fills the air.

Beatrice holds her hand to her mouth as she tries to make sense of what she's seeing.

"I silenced you once," the demon growls. "I'll do it again."

The Stranger races to scribe a crude circle in the floor around himself and the demon with his knife. "Malphas!" he declares again. "I command you to be gone!"

The demon laughs. "How long do you have, you squawking feathered pet of hags? A few hours? Until daylight? Only I can dispel the curse that was put on you long ago. Every time you speak my name, you weaken whatever magic is upon you now. If you stop this foolish game, I'll free you. Wouldn't you like to spend the rest of your days as a man instead of a lowly raven?"

Beatrice stares at the Stranger in disbelief. *A raven? How can it be?*

"Be gone, Malphas!" the Stranger cries once more as he lunges forward and sinks his dagger into the demon's side.

The demon reels and howls with anger and pulls out the weapon, dropping it in a clatter on the floor. Blood shines wet from the gash in his side as he clutches the young man by the neck and begins to strangle the life out of him.

Seeing the demon's victim suffer is more than Beatrice can bear. This is no stranger, this is the witches' beloved familiar. "Perdu!" she cries, rushing toward them. The demon turns his gaze on her, his grip squeezing even harder on the young man's throat. "I'll let him live, but only if you do as I say."

Perdu's face is turning pale, his body growing weaker by the second.

Beatrice straightens, and stares the demon down. "Tell me what you want."

"I merely want you to become all you're meant to be," the demon says, licking his scarred lips. "Haven't you grown tired of all the rules that bind you as a witch? I would never hinder you, never keep you from your destiny. I could give you powers of both dark and light: curses and spells; poisons and elixirs; all the minions of Hell at your command. Wouldn't that be exciting? With your gifts and my power we could rule the world, you and I."

His desire claws at her body as his need to possess her slithers through her mind.

"Don't hesitate, or he will pay," the demon growls, twisting Perdu's neck. "This is your last chance."

No, it's not, Beatrice vows as she grabs the dagger from the floor and puts it to her own throat. "Devil, devil, I defy thee."

The demon laughs.

Beatrice stands her ground. "Devil, devil, I defy thee."

The church bells of Madison Square begin to ring in anticipation of the New Year, their pious tolling echoing through the air.

"Run!" Perdu utters with his last breath.

And the demon hurls him through the glass.

Sweep the shadows from behind every door;
bring the demons into the light; confess
every secret, expose every lie, all before
midnight. Call to the woods and the spirits
of wild places, call to lost souls without rest
or home. Bid them to gather for the hour of

her reckoning, for the time of the Wild Hunt
has come.

The ballroom is consumed with the chaotic frenzy of revellers ready to welcome the New Year. Couples are locked in hungry embraces, gentlemen engaged in foul-mouthed shoving matches. Drunken guests gather around the stone well to drop their precious belongings inside it: rings, watches, jewelled necklaces and bracelets all tumble into the void. Brass horns and sleigh bells clamour in every corner as fireworks and gunshots from the park rattle the windows. Eleanor and Adelaide find each other in the crush, both unsuccessful in their search for Beatrice.

"What do we do?" Adelaide asks, fraught.

Eleanor frowns and shakes her head. "We go on without her and hope for the best. If he's got her, calling the hunt is her only chance."

Just then, Beatrice bursts into the ballroom, with the demon in frantic chase. As he makes one last lunge for her, a trio of the Baroness's footmen catch him with the points of their spears, threatening to stick him clean through.

Only a few of the guests even notice the curious turn, and those who do think it a clever entertainment. "Look at Krampus squirm!" one says as he points to the demon's horns and ghoulish fangs with great excitement. The rest are far too busy with love or war or New Year's cheer to pay attention.

While the demon seethes with frustration inside the circle of spears, Eleanor and Adelaide run to Beatrice's side. She's shaking, reeling from seeing Perdu's fate. She wants the demon to pay. There's no time to waste. *Let the Wild Hunt come and take him away.* Putting all her hope in magic, she joins hands with her sister witches so they can finish their rite.

Adelaide speaks first:

All good creatures of the wood who bear her sacred light,

> *Come by wind and winter's turn,*
> *When half spent is the night.*

She watches in amazement as every guest assumes the form of the animals on their masks. Stag, wildcat, bear and boar, lumber forth to pace and snort at the demon's feet.

Eleanor is next:

All strange folk who hidden dwell, in her magic rites,
Come by fire and sacred song,
When half spent is the night.

Her verse incites a rush of elves, trolls, goblins, gnomes, dryads, and fay-folk, who all work to bind the demon with chains and spider silk.

Beatrice, speaks last. Although her voice quakes with sorrow, it still carries:

All lost souls in need of comfort, care and delight,
Come by keening, tears and prayer,
When half spent is the night.

At her command, ghostly maids arrive by the dozens, accompanied by countless spirits from the parks and potter's fields of Manhattan. They wail and cry, laugh and howl, and with bucket, rag and broom, they wash away the ceiling—plaster and paint, rafter and beam—until all that's left is the night sky.

Save for the three witches, no earthly humans remain.

The room is filled with the cacophony of every strange being and spirit sounding their respective cries at once. It strikes such fear and awe in the witches' hearts that they dare not move or speak. As they stand in silence, a woman of light appears before them, dressed in a cloak of silver stars and a diadem of moonstone. She is the Baroness transformed, the Queen of Witches, the Mistress of Yule, the Mother of Lost Souls. With a wave of her sceptre, she silences all the creatures in the room.

"Bless you," she says to Adelaide, Eleanor and Beatrice. "Your faith has made me whole again so that I may take flight."

The women bow to her, amazed by her presence.

Waving her sceptre once more, the Queen of Witches signals for her retinue to assemble. As they go, the demon lets loose a long, anguished howl and the room is seized by a whirling mass of wind and snow. Demon, beast and spirit alike are taken up into the night sky, plucked away from earth as if they were as light as dandelion fluff. Closing their eyes against the tumult, the witches cling to one another in an effort to stay upright and together. They'd promised one another: *If one gets swept away, we all go.*

The Mistress rides but once a year across the night sky with her wild attendants racing beside her. She drives her phantom chariot from city to town, village to woodland, bringing light to those who have served her well. Woe to the liars, deceivers, and demons of the world, for her punishment is swift and harsh.

When the storm subsides at last, everything in the room except the three witches has disappeared.

6

JANUARY 1, 1882

The women walk home in silence, lost in their thoughts.

Adelaide resolves to begin the New Year by confessing all her secrets to Dr. Brody and accepting his proposal (if he'll still have her). *A June wedding would be nice,* she thinks. *Or perhaps May, in the park. Or next week, at City Hall. Why wait?*

Eleanor's mind is busy making a list of things she might take to Paris, should she decide to go. *Skirts, shoes, dresses. How cold is it there in winter?* With the demon out of the way, she won't need to worry (so much) over Beatrice.

Beatrice is doing all she can not to cry. She'd

seen no sign of Perdu, man or bird, outside the hotel. In the same strange way the ballroom had been returned to its former state, there'd been no broken glass on the sidewalk from the conservatory windows, no evidence that anyone had met with a terrible fall. She still doesn't understand all that Mr. Palsham had said about the curse he'd placed on Perdu, so it's hard to know how she can explain to Eleanor what happened to him. Clearly the Stranger had been in her dreams for a reason, but had it been the Baroness who'd put him there, or had Perdu worked some magic that was beyond her knowing?

Her heart aches at the thought that he could be gone for good.

As they approach Dr. Brody's house, a dark shape passes in front of a streetlight and settles on the stoop.

Beatrice stifles an astonished cry. She can't believe her eyes.

"How did you get here?" Eleanor says, scooping up her pet in her arms. "Did Mrs. Stutt put you out?"

"Someone's been a naughty boy," Adelaide teases as she opens the door.

Carrying Perdu inside, Eleanor sets him on the table in the foyer. She wags her finger at the raven. "Bad bird! You know better than to go out at night."

Beatrice comes to him, strokes his feathers and inspects him beak to tail.

"I am no bird," the raven chortles.

Leaning close, Beatrice looks him in the eye. "I know."

On New Year's Day, the city is beset with gossip about the ball. Many guests claim they woke up this morning snug in their bed (or someone else's) with no memory of how they got there. Others say the soles of their shoes were worn out by morning light.

One newspaper headline reads:

𝔑ew 𝔜ear's 𝔕evels 𝔊one 𝔚rong.

**Prominent Citizen Wentworth is found dead
in a 5th Avenue alley wearing a party mask,
his stomach slit and filled with straw.**

Mrs. Stutt becomes the lucky recipient of a personal note from the Baroness that includes a recipe for *Engelszopf.* "It's exactly like my *Mutter* used to make," she says, as she presents a fresh-baked loaf to the three witches after supper. "Just the scent of it makes me feel young again." The delicious treat has a most unusual effect, leading the housekeeper and Adelaide to sit in front of the fire with a bottle of schnapps long after Eleanor and Beatrice have gone to bed.

As the pair laugh and talk over past misunder-standings, a small calico cat comes to Beatrice's window asking to be let in. Before it can rouse the young woman from her dreams, Perdu taps three times on the glass and sends it away.

THE END

AMI McKAY's debut novel, *The Birth House*, was a #1 bestseller in Canada, winner of three CBA Libris Awards, nominated for the International IMPAC Dublin Literary Award, a finalist for Canada Reads and a bookclub favourite around the world. Her second novel, *The Virgin Cure*, a Best Book pick across numerous lists, was inspired by the life of her great-great grandmother, Dr. Sarah Fonda Mackintosh, a female physician in nineteenth-century New York. And with her third, *The Witches of New York*, also a national bestseller, she was recognized by the *Globe and Mail* as "one of the country's most beloved storytellers." Born and raised in Indiana, McKay now lives in Nova Scotia.

A NOTE ABOUT THE TYPE

Half Spent Was the Night has been set in Walbaum. Originally cut by Justus Erich Walbaum (a former cookie mould apprentice) in Weimar Germany in 1810, the type was revived by the Monotype Corporation in 1934. Although the type may be classified as modern, numerous slight irregularities in its cut give this face its humane manner. Walbaum also designed the black-letter-style Fraktur typeface, used here for the newspaper headline on page 91.